This Book Belongs To:

_____

Favourite Goodnight Stories

Brown Watson

ENGLAND

CONTENTS

The Three Bears

Once upon a time there were Three Bears who lived in a little house in the woods. One of them was a Little Small Wee Bear, one was a Middle-sized Bear, and one was a Great Big Bear.

They each had a bowl for their porridge. The Little Small Wee Bear had a little tiny bowl, the Middle-sized Bear had a middle-sized bowl, and the Great Big Bear had a great big bowl.

And they each had a chair to sit in. The Little Small Wee Bear had a little wee chair, the Middle-sized Bear had a middle-sized chair, and the Great Big Bear had a great big chair.

And also they each had a bed to sleep in. The Little Small Wee Bear had a tiny little bed, the Middle-sized Bear had a middle-sized bed, and the Great Big Bear had a great huge bed.

One morning, after they had made the porridge for their breakfast and poured it into their porridge bowls, the Three Bears went for a walk in the woods while their porridge cooled, for they did not want to burn their mouths by trying to eat it too soon.

While they were walking in the woods, a little girl whose name was Goldilocks came to the house. She looked in at the window and then she peeped in at the keyhole and, seeing nobody in the house, she lifted the latch and went in. There she saw the porridge on the table.

First she tasted the por-
ridge of the Great Big Bear,
and that was too hot.

Then she tasted the
porridge of the Middle-sized
Bear, but that was too cold.

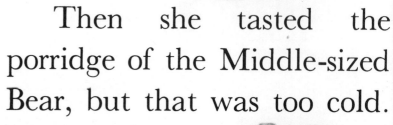

And then she went to the porridge of the
Little Small Wee Bear and that was neither too
hot nor too cold but just right, and she ate it all up.

Next Goldilocks went into the parlour and there she saw the three chairs. First she tried sitting in the chair of the Great Big Bear, but that was too hard. And then she sat down in the chair of the Middle-sized Bear, but that was too soft. But the chair of the Little Small Wee Bear was just right, and she sat in it until the bottom broke.

Then Goldilocks went into the bedroom where the Three Bears slept. First she lay down upon the bed of the Great Big Bear, but that was too high at the head for her.

Next she lay down upon the bed of the Middle-sized Bear, but that was too high at the foot for her.

And then she lay down upon the bed of the Little Small Wee Bear, and that was neither too high at the head nor too high at the foot, but just right.

So she covered herself up comfortably and fell fast asleep.

By this time the Three Bears had been walking about for some time in the woods and they thought their porridge would be cool enough now, so they came home to eat their breakfast.

Now Goldilocks had left the spoon of the Great Big Bear standing in his porridge, and he noticed it straight away.

"SOMEBODY HAS BEEN EATING MY POR-RIDGE!" said the Great Big Bear, in his great, rough, gruff voice.

And when the Middle-sized Bear looked at her porridge, she saw that the spoon was standing in her porridge, too.

"*SOMEBODY HAS BEEN EATING MY POR-RIDGE!*" said the Middle-sized Bear, in her middle-sized voice.

Then the Little Small Wee Bear looked at his porridge, and there was the spoon in his bowl as well but the porridge was all gone, every bit.

"SOMEBODY HAS BEEN EATING MY PORRIDGE, AND HAS EATEN IT ALL UP!" cried the Little Small Wee Bear, in his little, small, wee voice.

Now Goldilocks had not put the hard cushion straight when she rose from the chair of the Great Big Bear, and when he came into the parlour he noticed it straight away.

"SOMEBODY HAS BEEN SITTING IN MY CHAIR!" said the Great Big Bear, in his great, rough, gruff voice.

Goldilocks had pushed down the soft cushion in the middle-sized chair.

"*SOMEBODY HAS BEEN SITTING IN MY CHAIR!*" said the Middle-sized Bear, in her middle-sized voice.

"SOMEBODY HAS BEEN SITTING IN MY CHAIR AND HAS BROKEN THE BOTTOM OF IT!" said the Little Small Wee Bear, in his little, small, wee voice.

Then the Three Bears thought that they had better search through the rest of the house, so they went into the bedroom where they slept.

Now Goldilocks had pulled the pillow of the Great Big Bear out of its place, and he noticed it straight away.

"SOMEBODY HAS BEEN LYING IN MY BED" said the Great Big Bear in his great, rough, gruff voice.

And Goldilocks had pulled the pillow of the Middle-sized Bear out of its place.

"SOMEBODY HAS BEEN LYING IN MY BED!" said the Middle-sized Bear, in her middle-sized voice.

And when the Little Small Wee Bear came to look at his bed, there was the pillow in its right place, and upon the pillow was the golden-haired Goldilocks.

"SOMEBODY HAS BEEN LYING IN MY BED AND HERE SHE IS!" said the Little Small Wee Bear, in his little, small, wee voice.

When Goldilocks heard the little, small, wee voice of the Little Small Wee Bear, it was so sharp and so shrill that it awakened her at once. Upon seeing the Three Bears she ran to the window, and jumped out.

And whether or not Goldilocks ever found her way out of the woods and became a better little girl, no one has ever known. But the Three Bears never saw her again.

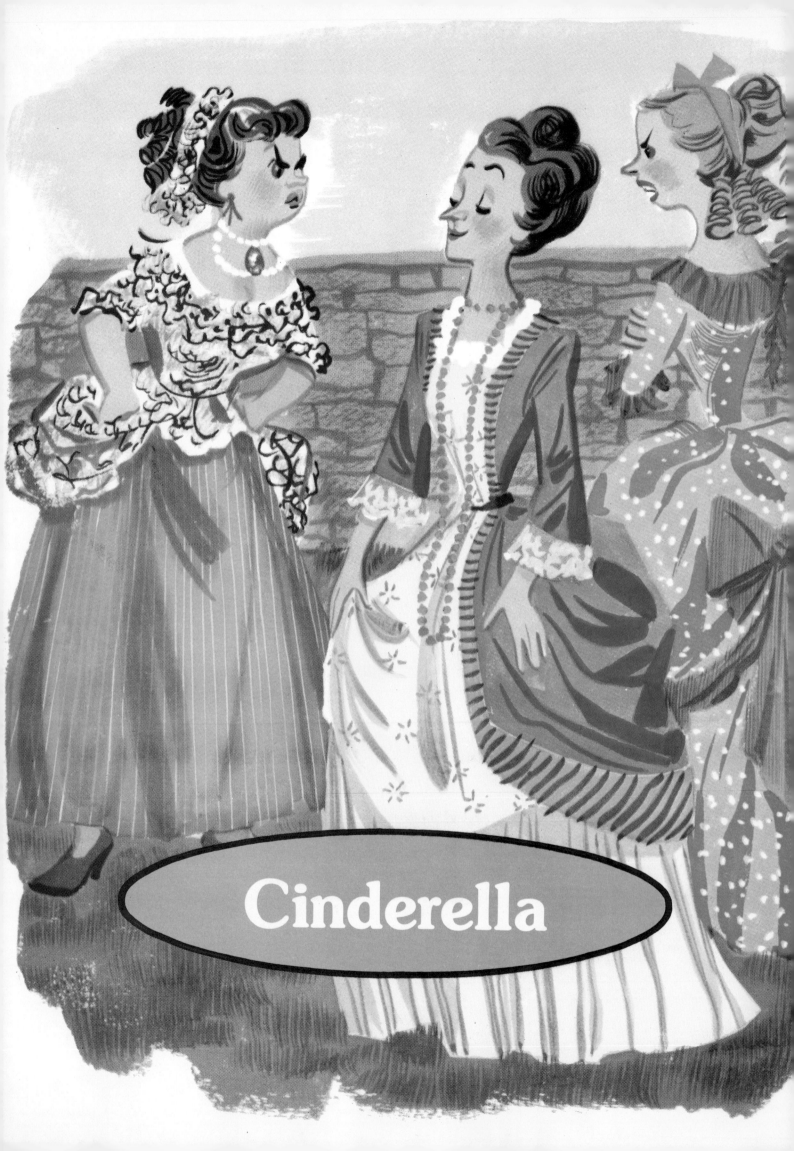

Cinderella

ONCE UPON A TIME there was a little girl whose dear mother died, and whose father married for his second wife the proudest and unkindest woman that ever was seen. She had two daughters who were exactly like her in every way. The little girl, however, was all sweetness and goodness.

The new wife could not bear the gentleness of the little girl because it made the sharp voices and selfish ways of her own daughters seem more hateful, and she put her to doing the hardest work in the house.

When the little girl's work was done, she used to cuddle down in the chimney corner in the ashes and cinders to keep warm. For this reason she was called Cinderella. And in spite of her ragged clothes, she was a hundred times prettier than her sisters in their elegant dresses.

One day the King's son gave a ball. Of course Cinderella's sisters were invited, because with their airs and graces they were very fine ladies indeed.

At last the happy evening arrived. The two sisters made ready for the ball. After their carriage left, Cinderella burst into tears.

Suddenly her godmother stood before her and asked what the trouble was.

"I want—I want," sobbed poor Cinderella, but the tears came so fast she could say nothing more.

"Do you wish you might go to the ball?"

"Yes," said Cinderella, with a deep sigh.

"Well, then," said her godmother, "I will see that you go. Run out into the garden and bring me a pumpkin."

Cinderella did not see what on earth a pumpkin could have to do with her going to the ball, but she ran quickly, chose the biggest pumpkin on the vines, and carried it to her godmother.

Her godmother touched it lightly with her ivory staff, and the pumpkin was changed into a splendid gilded coach.

Then she went and looked into the mouse trap, where she found six live mice. She told Cinderella to lift the door of the trap just a little, and as each mouse ran out she tapped it lightly with her staff, and at once it became a spirited steed. Altogether, they soon had a fine turnout of six prancing mouse-grey horses in bright, jingling harness.

But what to do for a coachman?

"I will go and see if there are not some rats in the rat trap," cried Cinderella. "We might make a coachman out of one of them!"

"Good!" said her godmother. "Run and see."

So Cinderella brought the rat trap. In it there were three big rats. The fairy chose the plumpest one with the longest whiskers, and changed him into a jolly fat coachman with the finest sweeping moustaches you ever saw.

Then the godmother said:

"Go into the garden and bring me the six lizards you will find behind the watering can."

Cinderella had no sooner brought the lizards than her godmother changed them into six foot-men. They jumped up behind the coach and sat there as stiff and straight in their gold-braided uniforms as if they had done nothing else all their lives. Then the fairy said:

"Now you have all you need to take you to the ball. Are you not happy?"

"Yes," faltered Cinderella, "but how can I go in these ragged clothes?"

The godmother just touched her with her staff, which was really a fairy wand, and in a moment

the rags were changed to a dress of gold and silver tissue embroidered with precious stones. And on Cinderella's feet was a pair of glass slippers, the most graceful little slippers in this world.

Cinderella climbed into her gilded coach, the chubby coachman cracked his whip, but before the fiery horses had sprung forward, her god-mother said to her:

"Remember, my child, you must not stay one minute after midnight. For if you do, your coach will change back to a pumpkin, your horses will be mice, your coachman a rat, your footmen lizards, and your beautiful gown the same old clothes you wore before."

The King's son, when he heard that a beautiful Princess whom no one knew, had come, ran down the steps to meet her. He gave her his hand as she alighted from the carriage and led her into the ballroom.

The young Prince led Cinderella to the seat of honour and begged for the next dance. She danced so gracefully that everyone admired her more than ever. When supper was served, the young Prince ate nothing, because he could not take his eyes off Cinderella, who seated herself near her sisters and shared with them the fruit and desserts which the Prince gave her. They were very much surprised at the kindness from this great and gracious lady.

The Prince stayed close beside her and whispered love words into her ear. Cinderella was so happy she quite forgot what her godmother had told her. When the first stroke of midnight sounded, she was sure it could not be later than eleven. But when she found it was really twelve, she sprang up and ran out of the ballroom like a startled deer.

The Prince hurried after her, but he could not overtake those flying feet. As she ran, Cinderella dropped one of her glass slippers, and this the Prince picked up most carefully.

Cinderella reached home all out of breath, without coach, without footmen, in the same sooty, ragged clothes she wore every day. All she had left of her finery was one little glass slipper.

When the two sisters returned from the ball, they told Cinderella about the beautiful lady who had been there. "But," they said, "as the clock struck twelve, she ran away so fast that she dropped one of her little glass slippers. The King's son found it, and all the rest of the evening he did nothing but look at it."

What they said was true. A few days later the Prince's messenger rode through the streets and blew a great blast on his long silver trumpet. Then he cried in a loud voice that the King's son would marry the maiden who could wear the glass slipper.

The slipper was tried first on the princesses,

then on the duchesses and court ladies, but it fitted no one. Finally it was carried to Cinderella's home and tried on the two sisters. Each did her best to squeeze her foot into it, but it was far too small.

Cinderella, who had been watching them and who knew her slipper, said with a smile:

"What if I were to try?"

Her sisters began to jeer at her, but the King's herald turned and looked at her closely. He saw even through the soot that she was beautiful and declared that it was only right that she, too, should try on the slipper. He knelt and held the little slipper to her foot, and it fitted her like a glove.

The sisters gasped with amazement, but they were even more surprised when Cinderella took the other slipper from her pocket and slipped it on her other foot. No sooner had she done this than her godmother appeared. She touched Cinderella with her wand, and there stood the Princess who had gone to the ball, but even more richly dressed than before. When the two sisters saw that it was really Cinderella who stood before them, they fell on their knees and begged her to forgive them. She lifted them up, kissed them, forgave them, and begged them to love her always.

She was led to the Prince, who thought her lovelier than ever and they were married soon after. And then because Cinderella was as good as she was pretty, she took her sisters with her to the palace, and there, after their tempers and manners had improved, she married them to two fine gentlemen of the court.

The Gingerbread Man

Once upon a time a little old man and a little old woman lived in a pleasant cottage behind a white fence. They were very happy, for their grandchildren lived nearby.

One day the little old woman was baking. When she had put her loaves of bread in the oven, she said to herself, "Now I shall make some gingerbread biscuits for my grandchildren."

So she made a lot of gingerbread biscuits. She put them onto a tray, and put the tray into the oven to bake.

"I have some gingerbread dough left," she said to herself. "I know what I'll do. I shall make a little Gingerbread Man." So she rolled out the dough, and very cleverly she shaped a little Gingerbread Man.

"Now to dress him up," said the little old woman. She sprinkled brown sugar over his round little body to give him a brown coat, and she stuck three big raisins in front for buttons. Then she gave him a pair of raisins for eyes and a little lump of gingerbread for a nose. His mouth she made with pink sugar.

She was pleased with him, and said,

"Ah, there, my little Gingerbread Man,
Now you're all ready to go onto the tray."

So on a tray she laid him, and popped him into the oven. Then she went about her work while the fire burned and the oven baked the little Gingerbread Man.

At last she opened the oven door.

"My goodness, what a fine Gingerbread Man!" cried the little old woman when she saw what a wonderful brown colour he was. "I'll just lay him in the cupboard to cool, and when the children come, they can eat him."

But when the little Gingerbread Man heard this, he stood up on the shiny tray and hopped right off onto the clean kitchen floor.

"No one shall eat me!" he cried, and ran toward the door on his sturdy legs, shouting,

"I can run away from you, I can.
'Cause I'm the little Gingerbread Man!"

The little old woman was so surprised she didn't know what to do.

"Stop! Stop!" she called.

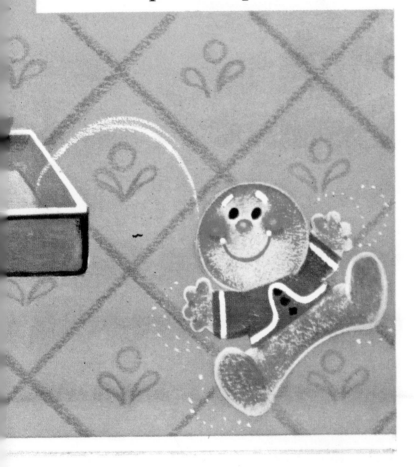

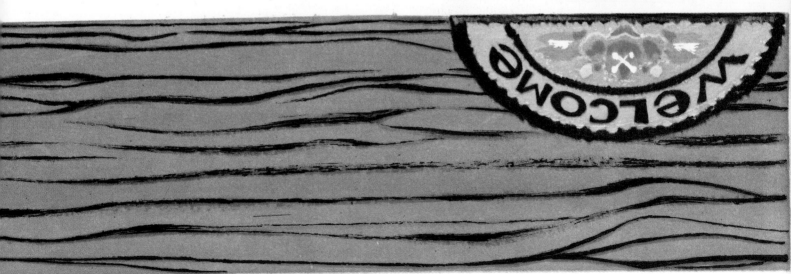

But the little Gingerbread Man ran on into the yard. Out in the garden the little old man was hoeing. When he saw the Gingerbread Man, he dropped his hoe and ran after him.

"Stop! Stop!" he cried, but the Gingerbread Man wouldn't stop.

He darted out through the gate in the white
fence, shouting,

"I can run away from you, I can.
'Cause I'm the little Gingerbread Man!"

And he ran down the road so fast that the little
old man was left far behind.

On and on he ran, and after a while he met a big black dog.

"Stop!" cried the dog. "Stop, and I'll take you home for my puppies to play with!"

But the little Gingerbread Man just laughed and called back,

"I can run away from you, I can.
I ran from the little old woman,
And the little old man.
And *you* can't catch me,
'Cause I'm the little Gingerbread Man!"

Nor could the big black dog catch him, though she ran until she was tired.

After a while the little Gingerbread Man met a big yellow cow.

"Stop!" she cried. "Stop, and let my little calf play with you!"

But he just laughed, and called back, "If you can catch me, I'll stop!"

The cow, however, was too wise to run after him, and soon he had left her far behind.

At last the Gingerbread Man ran past a big tall horse. The horse jumped a fence and ran along the road, too. He ran so fast—*rackety-rackety-rackety!*—that he soon caught up, and the little Gingerbread Man was frightened. But the horse said,

"This is the best race I ever ran!
What a runner you are,
Little Gingerbread Man!"

For the big tall horse just wanted to race.
And after a while, he turned back, saying,

"Run along, run along,
Little Gingerbread Man,
But beware of the fox,
For he'll catch you if he can!"

So the little Gingerbread Man ran on alone,
and thought what a fine fellow the horse was.
And at last the little Gingerbread Man ran around
a turn in the road—and who should be sitting
there but the fox!

"Good day," called the fox. "What a runner
you are! You must be tired from running so much."

But little Gingerbread Man stopped. Now that

he thought of it, his sturdy gingerbread legs *were* getting tired.

"My house is quite near," the fox told him, "and you can rest there, and eat dinner with me, too. Running must have made you hungry."

Now that he thought of it, the little Gingerbread Man *was* hungry. "How kind you are, Mr. Fox," he said.

"Just follow me, then," smiled the fox. And he led the way with the tired Gingerbread Man following at his heels.

"What a treat he will make for my little ones!" thought the fox. "They will lick the sugar from his coat, and pick out his raisin eyes, and then gobble him down." But of course he didn't say a word of this out loud.

When they were almost at the fox's house, a bird in a treetop saw them coming and sang out,

"Run! run! little Gingerbread Man,
For the fox will eat you if he can!"

Then the little Gingerbread Man stopped in his tracks and remembered what the big tall horse had said. "If you want to eat me," he called, "you must catch me first!" And away he ran, with the fox right after him.

But the little Gingerbread Man could run much faster, and he shouted,

"I can run away from you, I can.
I ran away from the little old woman,
And the little old man,
And a big black dog,
And a big yellow cow.
As fast as the big tall horse I ran.
And *you* can't catch me,
'Cause I'm the little Gingerbread Man!"

He ran on and on, and left the angry fox far behind. Past the big tall horse he ran, and past the big yellow cow, and the big black dog. When he came to the cottage of the little old man and the little old woman, he was very tired.

Just as he neared the white fence, a little girl and boy came through the gate. They were the grandchildren.

"Why, here's the Gingerbread Man that Grandmother baked for us!" they cried. "Let's catch him!" And after him they ran.

The little Gingerbread Man was glad. "I'll

be good, and let them catch me," he said to himself. "These are the children I was made for, and they shall have me, after all."

So the little Gingerbread Man ran so slowly that the children soon caught him. This was the best fate that could befall the little Gingerbread Man, don't you think?

Puss-in-Boots

ONCE UPON A TIME a miller died and left all he possessed to his three sons. But he had only these three things—his mill, his ass, and his cat.

The property was soon divided. The eldest brother took the mill. The second son received the ass. That left only the cat for the youngest, who could not be comforted for his bad luck.

"My brothers," said he, "will be able to earn a living, if they work together. But when I have eaten my cat, and made a fur collar of his skin, I shall die of hunger!"

The cat had heard all this. Coming up to his new master, he said, "Do not worry, Master. Give me a hempen sack, and have me made a pair of boots, so that the brambles may not tear my feet. You shall see that you have not fared so badly."

As soon as the cat had got what he asked for, he put on his fine new boots and hung the sack around his neck. Then he went off to the rabbit meadow. Inside the bag he put some bran.

Hardly had he lain down when a reckless young rabbit ran into the sack.

The cat now went to the King. He was shown the way to the King's audience chamber. Making a fine low bow to the King, he said, "Sire, here is a rabbit which my lord, the Marquis of Carabas, has bidden me bring you."

"Say 'thank you' to your master, and tell him I am much pleased," said the King.

A few days later the cat hid in a wheat field. This time two partridges walked into his bag. At once he drew tight the strings, and the birds were safely caught. These he presented to the King, as he had presented the rabbit. The King was delighted and gave orders that the cat should be given something good to eat.

Thus the cat kept on for two or three months.

One day he learned that the next morning the King was going to drive on the banks of the mill stream with his daughter, who was the most beautiful princess in the whole world. So the cat said to his owner, "If you will take my advice, your fortune is made. You have only to go bathing in the stream. I will show you where."

The cat's master could not see what good could come of that. Still, he did as Puss advised.

While he was enjoying his bath, the King passed by. Now what did Sir Cat do but begin to cry with all his might, "Help! help! The most honourable Marquis of Carabas is drowning!"

The King put his royal head outside the curtains of his carriage. As soon as he recognized the cat, he commanded his royal guard to run in haste to the aid of the most honourable Marquis of Carabas.

While they were dragging the Marquis out of the water, the cat drew near the royal coach. He told the King that thieves had come and carried away all his master's clothes. Now it was really the cat himself who had hidden them.

The King ordered his Royal Wardrobe Keeper to go and fetch some of the finest garments for the most honourable Marquis.

The fine clothing set off his good looks so very well that the King's daughter found him exceedingly to her taste. The Marquis of Carabas had no sooner looked at her two or three times than he liked her very much indeed. The King, noting this, asked the Marquis to join the royal party on its drive.

The cat went running ahead. On meeting some peasants who were mowing he said to them, "Good folk who mow, if you do not tell the King that this meadow belongs to the most honourable Marquis of Carabas, you shall be minced as fine as pie meat!"

When the King passed, he asked the mowers whose meadow they were mowing. "It belongs to the Marquis of Carabas," they all said, for they were frightened by the cat's warning.

"You have a noble inheritance," said the King to the Marquis.

At last Puss reached a great castle. The owner was an Ogre. He was the richest Ogre you ever saw, for all the lands through which the King had passed really belonged to him. The cat had taken pains to find out what special magic the Ogre could do. Now he asked if he could speak with the owner of the castle.

"I've been told," said Sir Cat to the Ogre, "that you can change yourself into any sort of animal—for instance, into a lion, or even into an elephant!"

"That is true," said the Ogre, crossly, "and to prove it you shall see me change into a lion!"

Puss was so frightened to see a real lion in front of him that he reached the roof in the twinkling of an eye and climbed out upon the gutters for greater safety.

When Puss saw that the Ogre had changed back again, he came down from the roof. He confessed to the Ogre that he had had a very great fright.

"I've also been told," said Puss, "that you can take the shape of the very tiniest animal; for example, a rat, or even a mouse. I'll admit that I think it quite impossible."

"Impossible!" roared the Ogre. "You shall see for yourself!" And instantly he changed into a mouse and began to run about upon the floor. No sooner did the eyes of Puss-in-Boots fall upon the mouse than he threw himself upon it and ate it up!

Now the King, as he passed by, noticed the mighty castle of the Ogre and wished to visit it. Puss-in-Boots ran out to meet the royal party. "Welcome, Your Majesty!" he said. "Welcome to the castle of the most honourable Marquis of Carabas!"

"How is this, Marquis?" cried the King. "This wonderful palace, too, is yours? Nothing can be lovelier than this courtyard. Let us see the inside, I pray you."

Following His Majesty, who entered first, they all went into the great hall. There they found

ready a luncheon which the Ogre had ordered to be prepared for friends.

After seeing the immense wealth of the Marquis, and having drunk his health, the King said to him, "There is no one, my dear Marquis, whom I should like better as my son-in-law. It rests only with you."

The Marquis, with a low bow, accepted joyfully the honour offered him by the King.

As for Puss-in-Boots, he became a great lord and hunted mice only when he wanted amusement.

The Elves and the Shoemaker

THERE was once a Shoemaker who, through no fault of his own, had become so poor that he had only enough leather left for one pair of shoes.

In the evening he cut out the leather,
intending to make it up in the morning.
Then he said his prayers and lay quietly
down to sleep.

In the morning he sat down to work, but behold, the pair of shoes was already made, and there they stood upon the table. The poor man was amazed and

took the shoes into his hand to look at them more closely. They were so neatly sewn that not a stitch was out of place, as if they had been made for a prize.

Presently a customer came in, and as he was very pleased with the shoes, he paid more than was usual. With the money the Shoemaker was now able to buy leather for two pairs of shoes.

By evening he had his leather shaped out. When he arose the next morning he was ready to work with fresh spirit. But just as before, the shoes were standing finished on his table.

He did not want for buyers either. Two men came in who paid him so well that he bought material for four more pairs of shoes.

Early the next morning he found the

four pairs finished, and so it continued. What he cut out in the evening was finished in the morning. This went on until the Shoemaker was a well-to-do man.

One evening, not long before Christmas, when he had cut out the usual quantity he said to his wife, "How would it be if we stayed up tonight to see who it is that helps us so kindly?" His wife was willing, and lighted a candle. Then they hid themselves behind some clothes hanging in a corner of the room.

As soon as it was midnight two little elves came in and sat down on the Shoemaker's table. They picked up the cut-out leather and began stitching, sewing, and

hammering so swiftly and lightly that the Shoemaker could not believe his eyes. They did not stop until the shoes were finished. Then they ran swiftly away.

The following morning the wife said,
"The little elves have made us rich, and
we must show our gratitude. They have
very little clothing and must be cold. I

will make a little shirt, coat, waistcoat, and trousers, and knit some stockings for each. And you shall make them each a pair of shoes."

The husband agreed and one evening, when all was ready, instead of cut-out leather they left the presents on the table. Then they hid to watch the results.

At midnight the elves came in, skipping about and eager to go to work. When they saw no leather, but the charming little clothes, they were astonished and delighted. They quickly put on their new outfits and, smoothing them down sang,

"Smart and natty boys are we,
Shoemakers we'll no longer be."

And so they went on hopping and
jumping over the stools and chairs, and at
last out of the door. They did not come
again, but the Shoemaker fared well in all
he undertook, and lived happily to the
end of his days.